MUMU?

David Mackintosh

HarperCollins *Children's Books*

MuMu is not quite MuMu today.

for
Charlie Lloyd
and the Animal
Kingdom

First published in hardback in Great Britain by HarperCollins Children's Books in 2015. 10 9 8 7 6 5 4 3 2 1
ISBN 978-0-00-746309-1   HarperCollins Children's Books is a division of HarperCollins Publishers Ltd.
Text and illustrations copyright © David Mackintosh 2015. Designed and lettered by David Mackintosh.
www.profuselyillustrated.com   The author/illustrator asserts the moral right to be identified as the author/
illustrator of the work. A CIP catalogue record for this title is available from the British Library.
Visit our website at: www.harpercollins.co.uk
Printed and bound in China.

MuMu's having a bad day, and it's not going to get any better.

8.00am

8.01am

8.12am

Sniff.

8.17am

8.21am

8.30am

8.42am

Cough.

8.55am

Sigh.

8.02am

8.05am

8.11am

8.24am

AHEM.

8.25am

8.29am

8.56am

Things are just that bad.

They certainly are.

NOTHING CAN PUT
THINGS RIGHT.

AND THAT'S THAT.

SO
THERE.

But I know
how to cheer
MuMu up.

I don't
think
so.

I know MuMu likes
shiny shop windows
and new things,

They won't have my size.

and the Blue Lake,
when the weather's
just right.

I don't want to get my hair wet.

Today is a little
cloudy. I guess.

I've probably seen it.

Films are MuMu's favourite.
Especially ones with horses.

Then, there are always
oysters and french fries.

I had a late breakfast.

I know everything MuMu likes to do.

Like getting out and about,
away from it all,
into the fresh air,
with the smell of the countryside.

SNIFF.
Hayfever.

Or a quiet game of hide and seek.

I'm not even counting, you know.

Better still, MuMu likes
exciting, noisy things
just as much.

It's too rattly.

At least,
that's what
I thought.

Of course,
MuMu loves salted peanuts,

and visiting a rose garden.

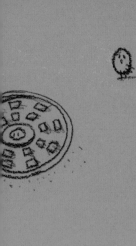
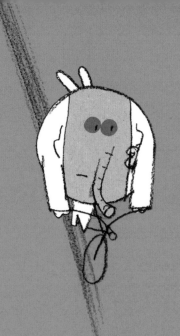

Now...
think,
think,
THINK...

OK...

What's needed is something new.
Something special and exciting
that will make everything look
better and put things right.

Something MuMu's
never tried before,
for a change.

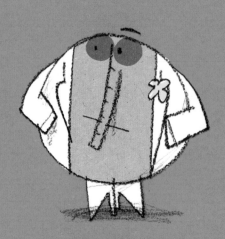

And I know just what that something is!

A something right around the corner.

My favourite and something that **ANYONE** would like...

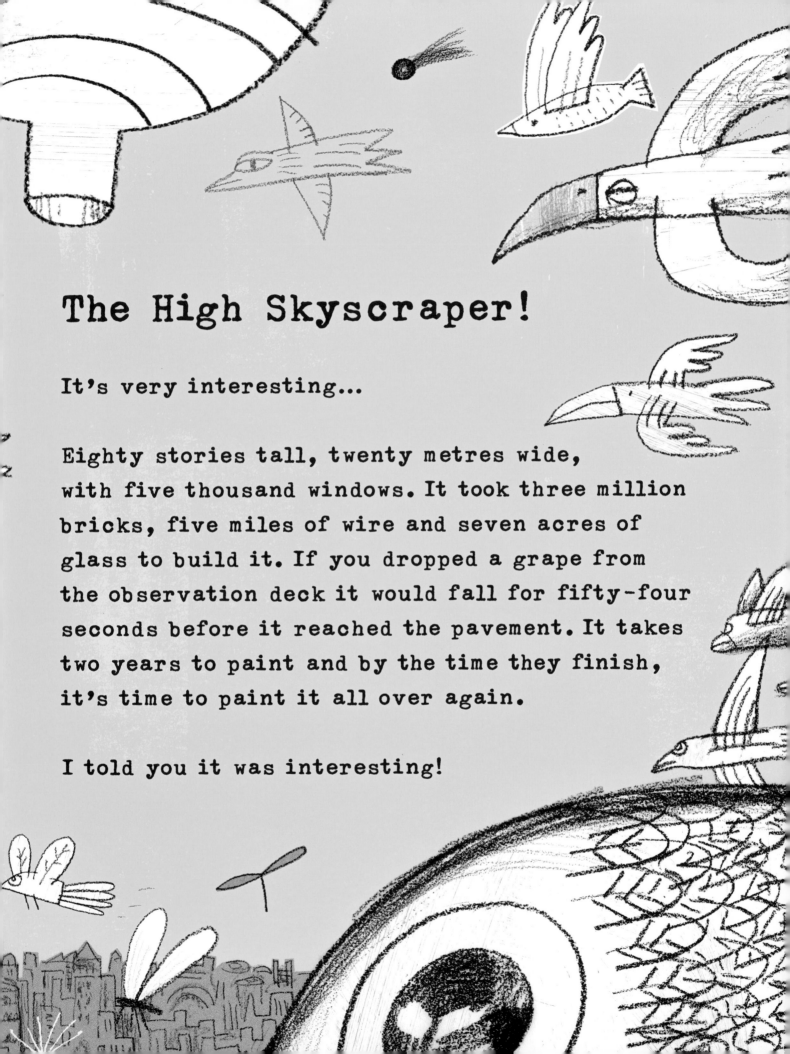

The High Skyscraper!

It's very interesting...

Eighty stories tall, twenty metres wide, with five thousand windows. It took three million bricks, five miles of wire and seven acres of glass to build it. If you dropped a grape from the observation deck it would fall for fifty-four seconds before it reached the pavement. It takes two years to paint and by the time they finish, it's time to paint it all over again.

I told you it was interesting!

When we get to the top all MuMu can say is...

It's
a bit
windy.

My legs are tired from running about all day.

MuMu's aren't.

And I'm a little out of breath.

MuMu's not.

You're just out of shape.

Hmmph!

MuMu's IMPOSSIBLE.

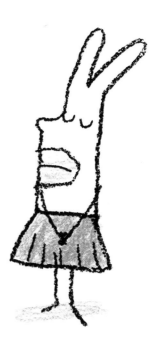

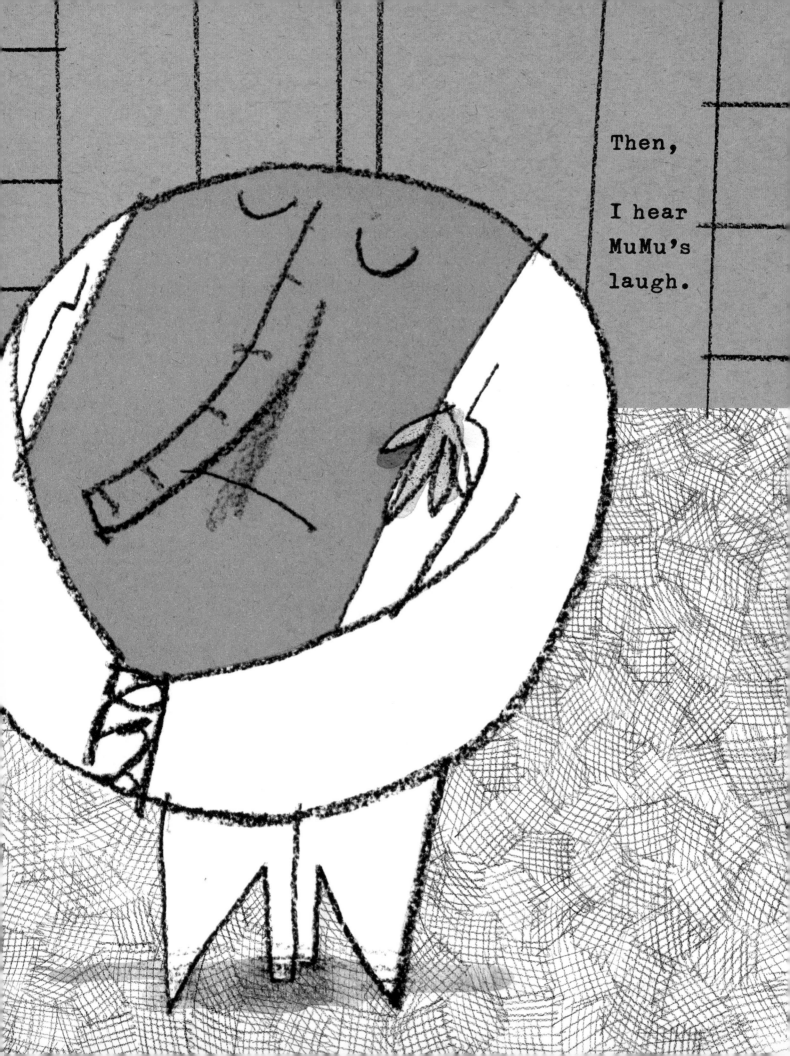

Then,

I hear
MuMu's
laugh.

Cheer up
Lox. It
can't be
so bad,
whatever
it is.

To help cheer me up,
MuMu decides I need a trip
to the Planetarium to look
at stars, because that's
something else I enjoy more
than anything.

Then I know MuMu is
feeling better.

And... we'll go to the Blue Lake and shopping on the way back.

Maybe it was magic that made
MuMu MuMu again?